For Quinn

And for everyone who has ever made a mistake

Dial Books for Young Readers

Penguin Young Readers Group

An imprint of Penguin Random House LLC

375 Hudson Street

New York, NY 10014

Copyright © 2017 Corinna Luyken

CIP Data is available

Printed in China • ISBN 9780735227927

10 9 8 7 6 5 4 3 2 1

Design by Lily Malcom

Text set in Perpetua

The art for this book was created using black ink, colored pencils, and watercolor.

With gratitude to ——

Steven Malk, who believed in this idea from the very beginning.

*And Namrata Tripathi and Lily Malcom, who contributed so many
good ideas to the making of this book.*

The Book of Mistakes

corinna luyken

Dial Books for Young Readers

It started

with one mistake.

Making the *other* eye even bigger
was another mistake.

But the glasses—

they
were a good idea.

The elbow and the extra-long neck?

Mistakes.

But the collar—

ruffled, with patterns of lace
and stripes—

that was a good idea.

And the elbow patches—

they were a good idea, too.

The bush was another good idea,

dark and leafy
so that you couldn't see through it . . .

to the frog-cat-cow thing.

Another mistake.

The big space
between the ground and the bottom of the girl's shoe—

was a little bit of a mistake, too.

But the roller skates?

Those were definitely *not* a mistake.

The second
frog-cat-cow thing
made a very nice rock.

And the girl,

with the very long leg,

looks like she always meant
to be climbing that tree.

Even the ink smudges
scattered across the sky

look as if
they could be leaves—

like they'd always wanted
to be lifted up

and carried.

And what about the girl?

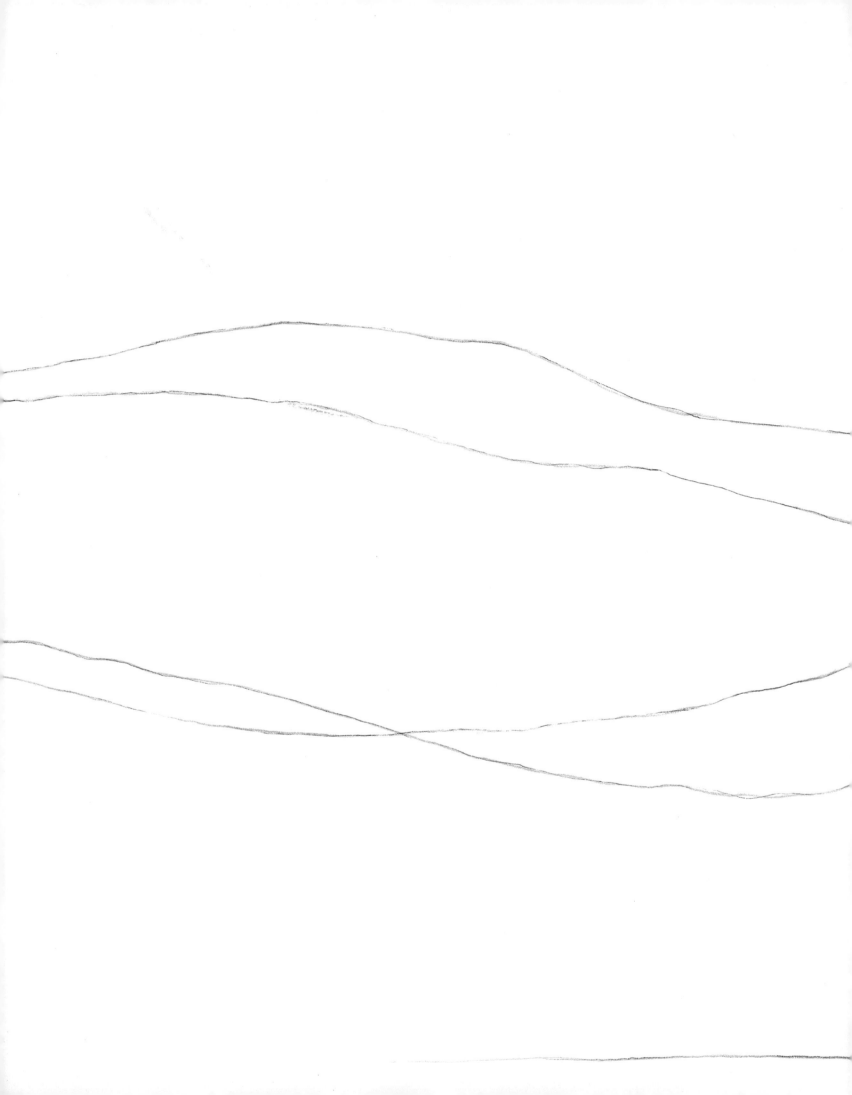

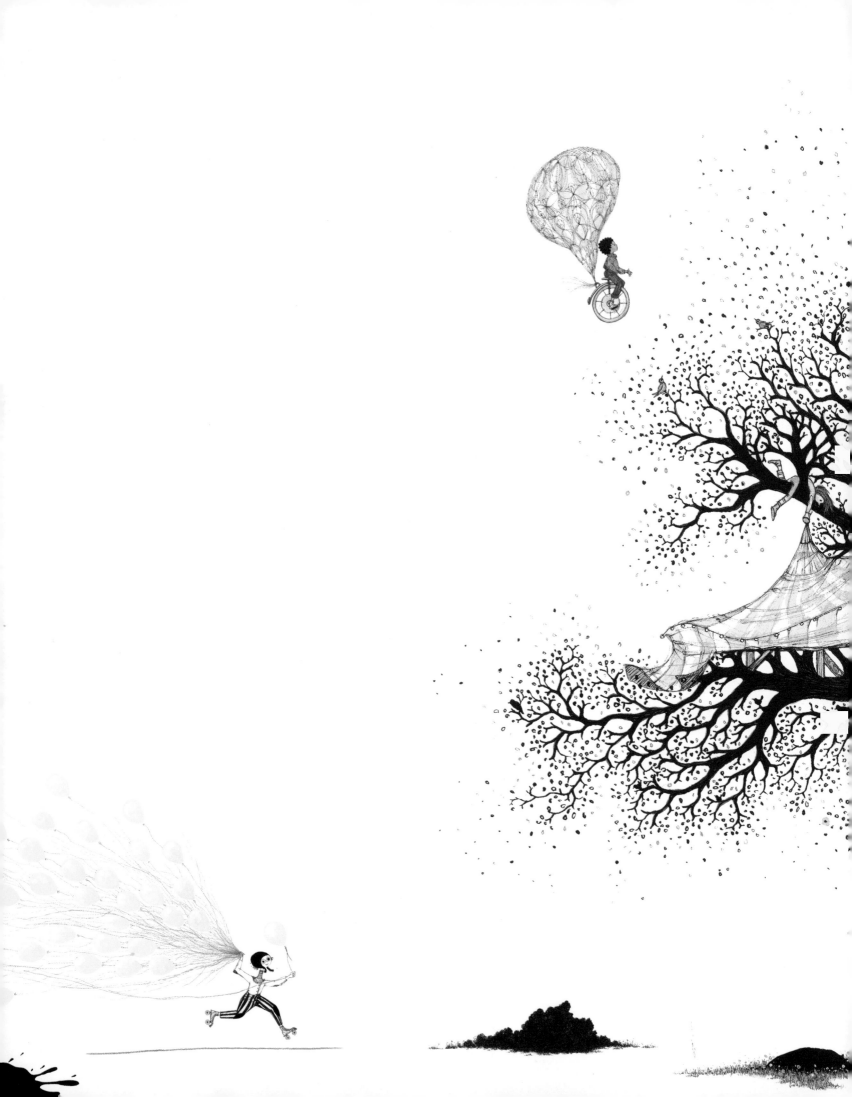

Do you see—

how with each
mistake

she is
becoming?

Do you see—

now

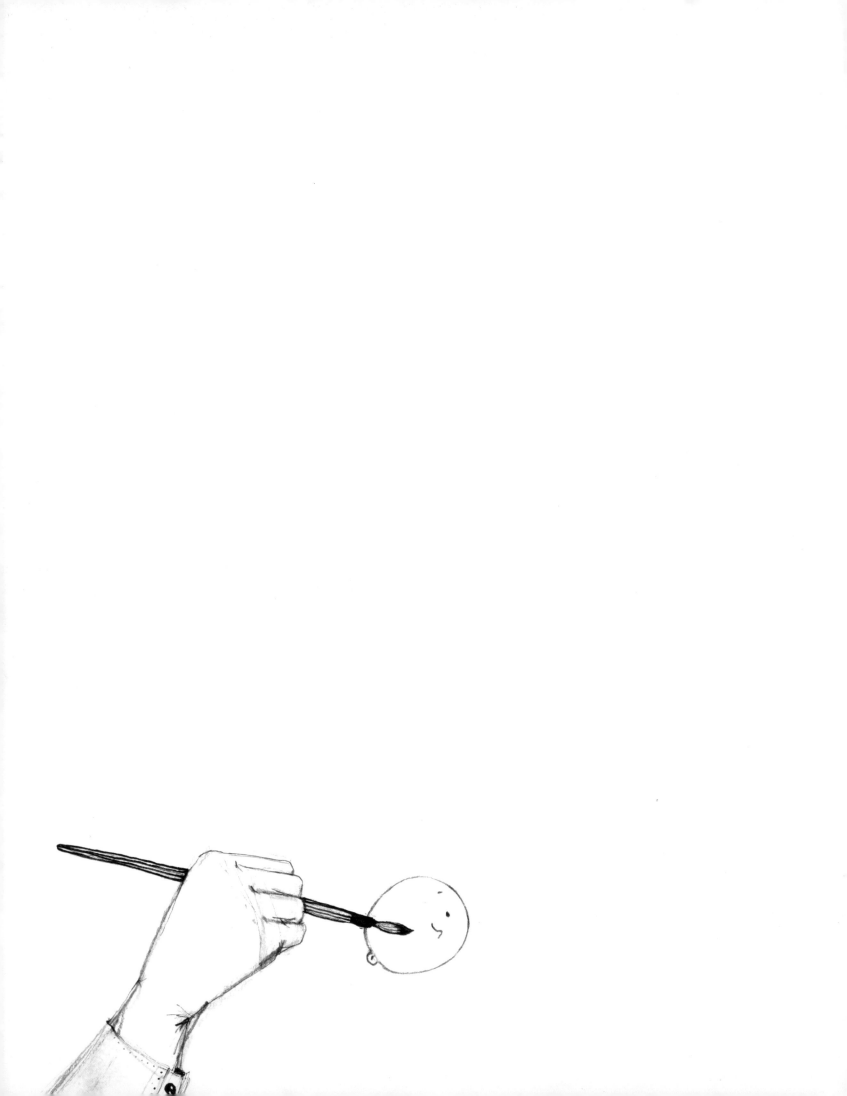

who she could be?